D0007307

Bricks for Breakfast

by Julia Donaldson
illustrated by Philippe Dupasquier

PICTURE WINDOW BOOKS
Minneapolis, Minnesota

Managing Editor: Catherine Neitge
Story Consultant: Terry Flaherty
Page Production: Melissa Kes
Creative Director: Keith Griffin
Editorial Director: Carol Jones

First American edition published in 2006 by
Picture Window Books
5115 Excelsior Boulevard
Suite 232
Minneapolis, MN 55416
1-877-845-8392
www.picturewindowbooks.com

First published in Great Britain by
A & C Black Publishers Limited
37 Soho Square, London W1D 3QZ
Text copyright © 2003 Julia Donaldson
Illustrations copyright © 2003 Philippe Dupasquier

Library of Congress Cataloging-in-Publication Data
Donaldson, Julia.
Bricks for breakfast / by Julia Donaldson ; illustrated by Philippe Dupasquier.
p. cm. — (Read-it! chapter books)
Summary: After winning a competition to design a new cereal and consuming
multiple bowls of it while shooting a television commercial, cereal-loving Stephen's
tastes change.
ISBN 1-4048-1275-X (hard cover)
[1. Cereals, Prepared—Fiction. 2. Contests—Fiction.] I. Dupasquier, Philippe, ill.
II. Title. III. Series.
PZ7.D71499Bri 2005
[E]—dc22   2005007185

Table of Contents

Chapter One

Stephen Rice loved cereal.

This was a typical day's menu for Stephen:

Breakfast—Cracklewheat

Playground snack—Corncrunch

Packed lunch—Sunnysnaps

Snack—Toastyoats

Supper time—Sugary Stars

Bedtime—Choc-o-not-hoops

Choc-o-not-hoops? What are they, you might be wondering. Well, Stephen's mom could tell you—she worked in a cereal factory. (Lucky Stephen!)

The company that Mom worked for was called Sunfield, and its most famous cereal was called Choc-o-hoops.

Mom's job was to watch the Choc-o-hoops coming out of the machine and pick out any broken ones. She was allowed to take the broken ones home. They were the Choc-o-not-hoops.

The only snag about the Choc-o-not-hoops was that they didn't have a box. Stephen loved cereal boxes almost as much as the cereal itself. Sometimes they had free prehistoric pencil tops in them.

Sometimes they had coupons to cut out, so you could save up for something really useful like a glow-in-the-dark skeleton.

What's more, the boxes were great
to read.

All in all, Stephen Rice was a happy
boy—until the dreadful day that Sunfield
closed down one of its factories. It was the
factory where Mom worked.

Chapter Two

Suddenly, they were poor. Mom was out of a job. There were no more free Choc-o-not-hoops. In fact, there wasn't any cereal, except for porridge, which didn't count.

The only way Stephen could ever eat any cereal or read any boxes was to get himself invited to friends' houses.

It was at his friend Bruce's breakfast table that Stephen read about the competition. This is what he read, on the back of a box of cereal:

DESIGN-A-CEREAL

Sunfield is inviting you to invent your own cereal and think of a name for it.
If we like the winning idea enough, we'll start making it. The winner will receive a free lifetime supply of the cereal.

There was a form for you to fill in.

Name:

Address:

Name of cereal:

Description of cereal:

Drawing of cereal:

"Can I cut this form out?" asked Stephen.

"No, my mom won't let us until the box is empty," said Bruce.

"That's not a problem," said Stephen, and poured himself another bowl of cereal. Three bowls later, the box was empty, and Stephen took the form home.

Chapter Three

Stephen chewed his prehistoric pencil top. He closed his eyes and hoped that a good idea would float into his mind. It didn't.

"Ricy Robots … Brontosaurus Bran …"

"Too difficult to make," said his mom, who was a bit of an expert.

"Snowflakes," he murmured.
"That sounds like a detergent," said
Bruce, who had come to visit.
"Well, you think of something, then,"
said Stephen.

But Bruce just suggested silly things like
Soggylumps and Grungygrain.

The closing date for the competition drew near. Two days before it, Stephen went to his school's Spring Fair.

He spent most of his pocket money on Fiberflake flapjacks and was just nibbling one when Mom appeared, clutching a purple vase.

"What a color!" said Stephen. "Did you fish it out of a pitcher of grape juice?"

"No," said Mom. "I bought it at the bric-a-brac stall."

"What's the matter?" she asked, for
Stephen was punching the air as if he'd
scored a goal.

"That's it!" he said. "Brick-a-Breck!"

Chapter Four

Stephen's mom sat in front of the television. The announcer of *Kidsnews* was talking.

"Eight-year-old Stephen Rice heard this week that he is the winner of Sunfield's Design-a-Cereal competition. Can you tell us about Brick-a-Breck, Stephen?"

"Yes. They're shaped like little bricks," said Stephen. "So you can build things with them before you eat them. Like this." He held up a picture. A cereal bowl with a castle in it filled the screen.

"Well," said the announcer, "Sunfield liked Stephen's idea so much that they've actually made some sample Brick-a Brecks—or should I say Breck-a-Bricks? —and here's Stephen with another idea."

Stephen appeared again with a bowl
with an igloo made of cereal bricks.
"These bricks are white because they're
coconut-coated," he said, "so I thought an
igloo would be a good idea."

"And what's the next step, Stephen?"

"Destruction," said Stephen, brandishing a milk pitcher. He poured milk onto the igloo, and it collapsed. Stephen was getting rather carried away. Some of the milk splashed on the announcer's tie.

"But aren't you sad to see your work destroyed?" asked the announcer.

"Oh no," said Stephen. "I just love eating cereal," and he started digging into the collapsed igloo.

"Stephen Rice, thank you very much," said the announcer, wiping his tie. "And now, on to the Brazilian rain forest. ..."

Chapter Five

Stephen's mom wasn't the only person watching *Kidsnews*. A man called Jasper saw it, too. Jasper was the director of a film company, which had been hired to make a TV commercial advertising Brick-a-Breck.

"That's the boy! He'll be perfect!" cried Jasper when he saw Stephen waving his spoon about.

And that was why a month later, Stephen and his pretend sister were sitting at a breakfast table in a television studio. The pretend sister was a rather annoying girl called Clare.

"What other commercials have you been in?" she asked. "None," said Stephen.

"I have," said Clare. "I've been in Supersoup and Great Big Softy toilet paper. This one's going to be easy as pie."

It did sound quite simple. The children had to pour milk on a Brick-a-Breck castle and ship and then eat them, while a little muscleman made of Brick-a-Breck did push-ups and danced on the table.

The script was:

Clare: *Castle- ruin*

Stephen: *Ship–wreck*

Brick-a-Breck man: *Build 'em up with
Brick-a-Breck!*

There was a lot of hustle and bustle in the television studio. Some people were scurrying around arranging things on the table, while others fiddled around with the big bright lamps.

Stephen was getting fidgety. This was taking ages. Even though he had eaten a fair bit of Brick-a-Breck during the rehearsal, he was beginning to feel hungry again.

At last, Jasper was
ready for Take 1.
A girl clapped a
clapperboard.

Clare, smiling
sweetly, placed
the last brick
on her Brick-a-
Breck castle and
said, "Castle."

Then she picked up
the milk pitcher,
poured milk on it
and said, "Ruin."

31

Now it was Stephen's turn. He placed the last brick on his ship and said, "Ship," then poured milk on it and said, "Wreck," as it collapsed.

After that, both children picked up their spoons and started to eat the cereal from their bowls.

"Cut," said Jasper.

Clare put down her spoon but Stephen finished eating his shipwreck. It was delicious.

Everyone else was crowding around a television, ready to see how Take 1 had turned out. Stephen joined them. One thing was puzzling him. "Where's the Brick-a-Breck man?" he asked.

"Don't be silly," said Clare. "He's a cartoon—they add him later."

Otherwise, everything looked fine to Stephen, but Jasper wasn't happy. "We need more shine on the orange juice," he said.

So a lighting man made one of the lights brighter, while the props people rearranged the milk pitcher and cereal box and brought a brand new castle and ship to the table.

"Take 2," said Jasper, and they went through it all again.

Afterward, when Stephen had eaten up the shipwreck plus Clare's ruined castle, which she didn't want, he joined the others around the television screen.

"Heaven," said Jasper, as his eyes lit on the gleaming orange juice. But as soon as Stephen's face appeared, he put his hand to his head. "That nose won't do," he said.

Clare giggled rudely.
"Too much shine," said Jasper.

Apparently, the light that made
the orange juice shine so brightly had the
same effect on Stephen's nose.
Stephen sighed as the makeup lady
dabbed his nose with a powder puff.

"What about Clare?" he asked.
"I'm not a red-nosed reindeer like you,"
said Clare. Stephen was getting fed up
with her. He hoped Take 3 would
be the last.

Chapter Six

Two hours later, Stephen was hoping Take 14 would be the last. This is what had happened ...

Take 3:
Stephen knocked the cereal box over.

Take 4:
A man from Sunfield arrived late and said there should be a bowl of fruit on the table to give a more healthy look.

Take 5:
The grapes didn't look shiny enough.

Take 6:
Someone said the purple grapes didn't go with Stephen's red T-shirt. Some green grapes were found instead.

Take 7:
Stephen's ship
collapsed before
he had poured the
milk on to it.

Take 8:
Clare wasn't
smiling enough.
(Stephen was
pleased that
she had done
something
wrong at last.)

Take 9:
Clare kicked
Stephen under the
table, and some of
the milk splashed
into the fruit bowl.

Take 10:
Jasper said
the table looked too
crowded and decided to
remove the orange juice.

Take 11:
The man from Sunfield
said he wanted the
orange juice back
and that it would be
all right not to have
the fruit bowl after all.

Take 12:
Stephen
wasn't looking
happy enough
while eating
the cereal.

Take 13:

Stephen wasn't looking rosy enough—
in fact, he was looking slightly green. Jasper
got the makeup lady to rub
some red stuff on his cheeks.

"I think they should have got Simon Jay to act
your part," Clare told Stephen.
"He was in Great Big Softy toilet paper with
me, and he was brilliant."

Just at that moment, Stephen wished that
Simon Jay, or anyone, could take his place.
There was a reason for his greenness:
He had eaten a whole fleet of Brick-a-Breck
ships and was feeling sick—or seasick,
maybe. His stomach, which Mom always
called a bottomless pit, now felt more like a
stormy sea.

"Take 14," said Jasper.

As Clare did her bit, the storm in Stephen's stomach grew stronger. He placed the last brick on the ship, smiled as brightly as he could, and picked up the milk pitcher for the 14th time. Just then, his stomach gave a gigantic heave, and instead of pouring milk on to his ship, Stephen was sick all over it.

There were no more "takes," except
for taking Stephen home.

In the studio, Jasper asked to see
Take 2 again—the one in which Stephen's
nose had been too shiny. This time,
Jasper said, "I like that shine!
It's healthy, it's natural, it spells
childhood! That's the one!"

Chapter Seven

Brick-a-Breck was a big success. Stores, cereal bowls, and tummies all over the country were full of it.

This was such good news for Sunfield that the company was able to reopen the factory in Stephen's town and give his mom her job back.

Actually, it isn't quite the same job. Instead of checking Choc-o-hoops, she has to check Brick-a-Brecks, and make sure they are all properly brick-shaped.

This means that instead of bringing back bags of Choc-o-not-hoops, she could bring back bags of Breck-a-not-bricks. But she doesn't, because Stephen, as the winner of the contest, receives a lifetime supply.

For some reason, though, Stephen has given up Brick-a-Breck. In fact, he has given up cereal altogether.

His latest craze is for pasta—shells, bow ties, tubes, spirals. He loves them all.

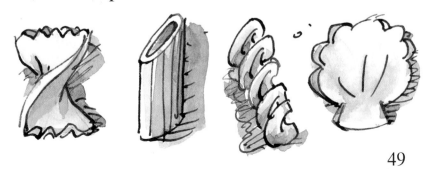

At this very moment, Stephen is poring over a box of Romeo's Pasta Ribbons and reading aloud …

DESIGN-A-NOODLE

Romeo's is inviting you to design your very own pasta shape.

About the author

Julia Donaldson has worked for many years as a performer and songwriter. One of her songs was made into a book, which led to her current career as a best-selling author.

Look for More *Read-It!* Chapter Books

Duncan and the Pirates by Peter Utton

Hetty the Yeti by Dee Shulman

Spookball Champions by Scoular Anderson

The Mean Team from Mars by Scoular Anderson

Toby and His Old Tin Tub by Colin West

Looking for a specific title or level? A complete list
of *Read-it!* Chapter Books is available on our Web site:
www.picturewindowbooks.com